KU-418-341

A Note from the Author

I've always been fascinated by worlds within worlds. Growing up in London, I often visited the National Gallery and one of my favourite pictures was of a couple who were looking in a mirror in which you could see them reflected in another mirror, in which the couple were looking in another mirror . . . and so on, with the mirrors and the pictures in them getting smaller and smaller into the distance. And so I felt pleased when I had the idea of writing a book about someone reading a book about someone reading a book.

When I began, I didn't know what all the books would be, only that one of them should be a library book, because I am a great fan of libraries, which is where so many of us discover our own favourite books. But I did know that I wanted to write in rhyme and I decided that each double page should end, "Inside his (or her) favourite book". Picture books usually have twelve double pages, so I needed eleven rhymes for the word book. Quite quickly I hit on Cook, Hook, Look, Shook, Brook, Rook, Crook, Took, Nook. But that was only nine. I was two short! I could have used "stook", meaning a sheaf of corn, but I didn't think many children (or even adults) would know that word. So I felt stumped . . . until I suddenly realised that there were other things you could read as well as books, which helped me come up with the remaining two rhymes: magazine/Queen, and encyclopedia/greedier (I must admit I was pleased with that one).

I imagined at first that the publisher might find twelve different illustrators – one for each book-within-a-book. But I'm glad now that they didn't take me up on that idea, because Axel did such a brilliant job making each book look different. I love the way that in the illustration of the crocodile story Axel has included a scribble to show that the crook (who is reading it in prison) is counting the number of days left before he is let out. I had to laugh at one book signing I did when a mother who had bought *Charlie Cook's Favourite Book* came back to complain, "Someone's been scribbling on this copy."

I have written a song to go with this book. It's called "The World Inside a Book" and it's the kind of song where you can make up your own verses about the books you like best. There isn't room to print the words and music here, but you can find it inside another book called *The Gruffalo's Child and Other Songs.*

Julia Donaldson

July 2014

SHIVER ME TIMBERS

FAIRY TALES
FROM A FORGOTTEN ISLAND

THE BEARO ANNUAL

JOUST JOKING!

STORIES of
REAL BIRDS

 For Alice, Alison and Alyx

First published 2005 by Macmillan Children's Books
This edition published 2015 by Macmillan Children's Books
a division of Macmillan Publishers Limited
20 New Wharf Road, London N1 9RR
Basingstoke and Oxford
Associated companies throughout the world
www.panmacmillan.com

ISBN: 978-1-4472-7678-4

Text copyright © Julia Donaldson 2005, 2015
Illustrations copyright © Axel Scheffler 2005, 2015

The right of Julia Donaldson and Axel Scheffler to be identified as the
author and illustrator of this work has been asserted by them in accordance
with the Copyright Designs and Patents Act 1988.

All rights reserved. No part of this publication may be reproduced, stored in or introduced into a retrieval
system, or transmitted, in any form, or by any means (electronic, mechanical, photocopying, recording or
otherwise) without the prior written permission of the publisher. Any person who does any unauthorised act
in relation to this publication may be liable to criminal prosecution
and civil claims for damages.

1 3 5 7 9 8 6 4 2

A CIP catalogue record for this book is available from the British Library.

Printed in China

Charlie Cook's Favourite Book

Julia Donaldson

Illustrated by Axel Scheffler

MACMILLAN CHILDREN'S BOOKS

Once upon a time there was a boy
called Charlie Cook
Who curled up in a cosy chair
and read his favourite book . . .

About a leaky pirate ship
which very nearly sank
And a pirate chief who got the blame
and had to walk the plank.
The chief swam to an island
and went digging with his hook.

At last he found a treasure chest,
and in it was a book . . .

About a girl called Goldilocks,
and three indignant bears
Who cried, "Who's had our porridge?
Who's been sitting on our chairs?"

They went into the bedroom,
and Baby Bear said, "Look!
She's in my bed, and what is more,
she's got my favourite book . . ."

ABOUT SIR PERCY PILKINGTON, A BOLD AND FEARLESS KNIGHT, WHO TOLD THE DRAGON...

Wait! I'm not quite ready for the fight.

You must hear this one first!

AND THEN HIS ARMOUR CLANKED AND SHOOK

AS HE READ ALOUD A JOKE HE'D FOUND
(INSIDE HIS FAVOURITE BOOK)...

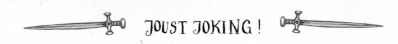
About Rowena Reddalot,
  a very well-read frog,

Who jumped upon a lily pad

and jumped upon a log,

Then jumped into the library
  which stood beside the brook,

 And went, "Reddit! Reddit! Reddit!" as she jumped upon a book...

About an oak tree full of birds.
Each bird had built a nest
And they had a competition
to decide which one was best.

They chose an owl to judge it,
and the winner was a rook
Whose nest was lined with pages
from his very favourite book . . .

About a girl who saw

a flying saucer in the sky.

Some small green men were in it

and they waved as they flew by.

She tugged her mother's sleeve and said,

"Look, Mum, what I've just seen!"

But Mum said, "Hush, I'm trying to read

my favourite magazine . . ."

About a wicked jewel thief
who stole the King's best crown

ADVERTISEMENT

Doctor Foster's

Patented Galoshes!

NEW!

"I never go to Gloucester
without them!"
says a delighted Doctor Foster.

**But then got stuck
behind some sheep,
which slowed his
car right down.**

**The King dialled 999
and soon the cops
had caught the crook,**

SITUATIONS
VACANT

⌘

GOVERNESS required for
Lady Mary, aged 7. The child
is sadly quite contrary. She
insists she sees aliens in the
garden. A strict governess is
required, who can curb this
vivid imagination.

   Apply with references to
Lady Fotherington, The Old
Rookery, Banbury Cross.

**And flung him into prison,
where he read his favourite book ...**

PRISON LIBRARY
DO NOT DAMAGE

About a greedy crocodile

who got fed up with fish

And went on land to try to find

some other kind of dish.

He went into a bookshop
and he there grew even greedier

While reading (on page 90
of a large encyclopedia) . . .

CAKE: a mixture of nice things, usually baked in the oven. It is eaten at teatime and on special occasions like birthdays and Christmas.

THE QUEEN'S BIRTHDAY CAKE

It took six lorries to carry the Cocoa Munchies for the Queen's birthday cake to the palace. The cake also required 4,276 bars of chocolate and 739 sackfuls of marshmallows. The special outsize cake tin was made by the Royal Blacksmith, using 2,647 melted-down horseshoes.

FAMOUS CAKE-EATERS

Britain's most famous cake-eaters are the Bunn twins of York. At the age of six they became the youngest ever winners of the York Festival Cake-Eating Competition. Aged ten, they had to be taken to hospital after knocking each other out, while both reaching for the same slice of cake. (Their dog then ate the cake.)

Abdout the biggest birthday cake the world had ever seen. A team of royal cakemakers had made it for the Queen.

The cake was so delicious
        that a famous spaceman took
A slice of it to Jupiter.
        He also took a book . . .

About a ghost who glided
round a castle every night,

Carrying her head and
giving everyone a fright.

She kept it up till morning,
then she found a shady nook

And put her head back on again
to read her favourite book...

About a cosy armchair,
and a boy called Charlie Cook.

SHIVER ME TIMBERS

FAIRY TALES
FROM A FORGOTTEN ISLAND

THE BEARO ANNUAL

JOUST JOKING!

STORIES of
REAL BIRDS

The pirate chief inside this story
used to look very different.
So did his parrot!